I0738010

Snow White
- the Real Story

by

Fred Zimmerman

art by Janice Appel

Introduction

I would like to thank several people without whom I am not sure this story would have been completed. Oh, I wrote the whole thing alright, but getting it from the first draft to its finished form was more than I could do alone.

So, Thank you, my best friend and wife Lauric H. Zimmerman, our great friend and illustrator, Jan Appel, my sister Margaret Z. Reed, Irma Sheppard, Karl Moeller, Debbie and Ken Blackman and Meher Baba.

I awoke one morning in 2014 from a deep sleep with three characters names on my lips. I promptly wrote them down knowing I had to do something with those wonderful names and, eventually, started to rewrite the story of Snow White in which, naturally, they became a part.

For a long period of my life as a performer, mime, dancer, and actor, I spent a great deal of time creating material that often became part of a performance. At one point, I became interested in recreating fairy tales on stage, with the thought of making most of the characters people of color. I didn't think it was fair that in almost all, if not all, of the fairy tales I grew up with the characters were white, and I felt it would be interesting to recreate these classics with black performers. Now, as a writer, I've taken the liberty to make Snow White a person of color.

****

This is a story of a family. The mother a Queen, once a princess from Africa, the Father a King from southeastern Europe, and a beautiful daughter.

Tragedy overcome with
love, friendship and discovery.

The Beginning

What good fairy tale wouldn't begin with "Once Upon a Time?" But wait, we're already way past that. Let's jump ahead, a bit before the moment when Snow White takes that FATEFUL BITE OF APPLE.

Snow White, known as Snow to friends and family, as you may recall, had escaped from the hunter who, at the request of her stepmother, had taken her into the woods to kill her. You see Snow White was to become Queen in a year or so when she was to come of age. Unfortunately for Snow White, her greedy, evil stepmother wanted to be queen.

After she freed herself, Snow spent several days wandering through the forest finding a few berries and the occasional root she could eat without getting sick. She also found water to drink that wasn't stagnant and managed fairly well to keep herself alive until, filthy and bedraggled, she found herself at a small stone cottage. After knocking several times, she poked her head inside and called, "Hello" a few times before she stepped in. Cautiously looking around, she ate a biscuit she found on a long wooden table and then curled up on one of the largest of the seven beds and promptly fell into a deep and dreamless sleep.

Not far from the cottage there was a mine that was being worked by seven brothers who happened to be Little People, commonly referred to as Dwarves.

At the end of a long day, after having to break through a rather hard vein of granite on the way to a small lode of silver, the owners of the house came home to a stranger, and a big person at that, in one of their beds. Well, she wasn't really a big person, for a big person would be a Giant. She was more normal-sized, so we will just call people of average height for the time, "Normals." For the time being, they decided to leave her be but didn't plan on letting her stay.

About a day later she awoke with seven small people sitting around her with frowns on their faces.

"Good evening!" one of them said, "Who are you and what are you doing here?"

Snow told her story, not telling them that she was a princess, but including the part about her deceased father and inhumanly nasty stepmother, making sure they knew she couldn't go back even if she knew the way.

The Seven had a family conference and decided as long as she was willing to do her share of the work around the house, she would be allowed to stay, for the time being. As time went by, she did her share and more. She even learned some hunting skills and gardening and eventually became like one of the family.

As we know, she was beautiful. That was what started all the trouble in the very beginning. What we didn't know, is that she was also kind, extremely intelligent and amazingly open-minded, for her time. She always saw people for who they were and was not turned off by the color of their skin, their parentage, or say… their size. So, when she found herself falling for the shy brother, Percival, for that was his given name, there were no mental hang-ups to get in the way of a budding romance.

 Two people couldn't have been more in love. They would meet surreptitiously behind the cottage after his workday had ended and before she served the Seven their evening meal.

The others knew what was going on but didn't let on and couldn't have been more pleased that their brother was in love with and loved by a Normal.

However, deep down, they didn't think it could end well. After all, she was considerably taller, and her stepmother was not a very nice person. She was evil, most definitely, but was she a witch? That's hard to tell and, for now, we'll leave witches for other fairy tales.

Snow and Percival had their differences. She was tall and after all, he was a Dwarf, a young, good-looking dwarf, but a dwarf all the same. Just holding hands had its difficulties, but they managed.

Their long afternoon walks on their favorite path in
the woods had a stopping place where there was an
opening with an amazing vista. There the mountains
in the distance seemed to come together in such a
way that, no matter the time of the year, the sun
would set between them. They would sit on some
logs that were ornately carved into a bench, watch
the sunset and recite poetry from the writings of the
renowned romantic poet of the day, Tomahachi.

I am beguiled by you,
I am in wonder of your love,
For life itself
Inspired me to be
Worthy of your love.
Let me be the slave of your love,
So that I can learn to become
A master of love for you.

Meanwhile, trouble was brewing, literally. Snow's stepmother was having another set-to with the enchanted mirror. You remember the mirror, don't you?

The stepmother spoke to the mirror in rhyme, or else the mirror wouldn't answer.

> Mirror, mirror in the frame
> Let's restart this number game.
> In a count from one to ten,
> Tell me, how lovely I am again.

The Mirror responded.

> Thou art, surely, an easy ten.
> I'll tell you that again and again.
> But Snow White, in the dimming glow,
> Is lovelier than you, ten times ten.

"What??? But she's dead!!" she screamed.

"No" said the mirror, "She yet lives, in the wood with seven around her."

It was then she began brewing the poison for the apple of choice and planning the method of its delivery.

Okay, now let's bypass the inevitable long years of "not quite dead" in the glass coffin, when this great-looking, totally self-absorbed prince comes along with the notion that he, alone, could save the now legendary sleeping beauty with his kiss. Who knows where he got that idea?! I mean who, in his right mind, thinks that a kiss could awaken someone from a catatonic state? He must have been reading too many fairy tales. The fact is, Snow was put in a type of suspended animation that ended when he bent over to kiss her causing a spark of static electricity to strike her face, ending her, uhhh... static state. Well, it's as good an explanation as any other!

Let's quickly move on and, it must be pointed out that, all this time Percival had watched lovingly over Snow as she lay motionless in the glass coffin.

We know that Snow awakened upon the delivery of the historic kiss, and the conceited Prince assumed it was her love for him that brought her back to life. He also thought the love he saw in her eyes was for him.

Of course, she was looking at Percival who was standing behind the prince in optimistic and eager anticipation of her awakening and returning to him. Without warning or a word being spoken, the Prince swept the still groggy Snow up onto his horse.

Percival was bursting with joy as Snow awakened
with love in her eyes, but that same joy was crushed
as he watched the love of his life being taken away,
against her will, kicking and moaning the whole time.
He immediately gave chase, yelling at the top of his
lungs until the Prince turned and, with his sword
drawn, threatened him with dire consequences if he
didn't cease his pursuit.

The Prince then turned his horse taking Snow home
to his kingdom where his family began plans for a
royal wedding.

At the point of waking, Snow moaned and gurgled a
little, which the Prince took to be moans and gurgles
of joy, but, after being almost dead for so long, it was
merely befuddlement and confusion. It was, actually,
a couple of weeks before Snow could speak and make
any sense at all. It was then that her protestations
began which, of course, the family dismissed as her
recuperation from a stagnant brain.

So, there she was, being held against her will by a
family she didn't know and was rapidly learning to
dislike intensely.

Meanwhile, back in the woods . . .

Downtrodden, Percival returned to his brothers and desperately yelled, "We have to go get her!" Of course, they didn't know what they could do, but they left with him, all the same. After two days of hard travel through hill and dale, they came to the castle and were refused entry. To make matters worse there was a huge sign at the gate which read

"NO DWARVES!"

This didn't stop them, but when they were met by armored men with swords and spears, what could they do? Well, they sent in a formal request for a hearing! to which they received arrows shot between their legs and a snarling promise that the next ones would land "between your eyes!"

Alas! Now what could they do? I'll tell you. They went back to the cottage, gathered a thousand Dwarves and hundreds of sympathetic Normals, donned armor, set up a siege on the castle, killed the family, freed Snow and returned to a peaceful life in the woods where they raised a passel of kids and lived a long and..... oh, wait.... that was Percival's fantasy. There were probably only about three or four hundred Dwarves within a thousand miles and maybe only twenty Normals who wouldn't cross to the other side of the street to avoid them. However, they did need to come up with some sort of plan. And back they went to the cottage, brainstorming all the way. This is the plan they made: Five of the brothers would stay behind to work the mine while Percival and Stupid (the smart one) whose real name was Albert (where do you think Einstein's parents got the idea?) would journey to Agar, the capital city of the empire, to seek assistance from other dwarves they knew who lived there.

A digression, if you don't mind, you may wonder why Albert was given the nickname, Stupid. Thank you for your curiosity. I will tell you why. Albert Miner's IQ was around 185. His genius mind worked at such a rate and his resulting behavior was so strange that he often seemed quite featherbrained. Over time, family and friends realized that he was much more intelligent than the rest of them, but the nickname ironically stuck. The combination of his intelligence and his behavior made him the ideal companion to make the trip with Percival.

We now must digress a little more to meet four more
of our principal characters by way of an introduction
to The Emperor, who also has, as you may have
guessed from his title, a significant part to play in our
story.

Somewhere between Cee and Kyzylorda, Vilnius to
the north and Trikala to the south, there was the
Empire of Agaragar. This Empire of Agaragar
consisted of five known Kingdoms, each ruled by a
King or Queen who in turn were all overseen by an
Emperor. To the west of Agaragar was a great sea.
The north and east were surrounded by mountains.
The interior consisted of beautiful and terrifying
forests where citizens lived, worked and played in
small family enclaves and villages. The south was
arid and covered mostly by desert.

Many goods, from a variety of food stuffs to common
and precious gems and metals, were traded among
the citizens of the five Kingdoms. The finest of these
were jewelry of silver, gold and platinum made by
skilled dwarf artisans. Dwarves also managed to

figure out over generations how to refine hemp into a cloth that was finer than silk and much more durable. You can imagine how in demand that was by the rest of the population. Mainly the population was made up of Normals. Many of the Dwarves used the term "Normals" as a derogatory slur. Today we might think of the Normals of that time as diminished in size by comparison to the present time, but we would be too nice to notice. However, some of us might treat them as badly as the Normals treated the dwarves in their time. There were also small enclaves of Giants who lived somewhere in the mountains and who rarely mixed with the other communities.

At the time of our story, Dwarves were treated quite poorly by most of the Normals. It is only reasonable that they only traded or befriended people, including a few Normals, with whom they had formed trusted friendships and business relationships.

 The caretaker of the Empire Agaragar at that time was known as "Fergie the Just." Until then there had been no formal "Justice System." Wait a minute, Fergie, the Just, you say? Yes, Emperor Reginald Ferguson the First. After a long line of ghastly or mediocre emperors before him, Fergie the Just was not only the first of that name but the first Emperor who actually paid any attention to his subjects and truly cared for them. Fergie was just a young ruler at the time of this tale and still experimenting and unformed in his thinking about how to make his kingdoms fair for all subjects, from peons to princes. You see, past emperors figured that keeping one kingdom from attacking another by means of brute force was enough. As far as interpersonal conflicts, there were no real courts, no judges and almost no lawyers. Yes, I said "almost."

Beginning in the year 372, the third year of Fergie's reign, there was a three- year period of great and terrible storms coming out of the western sea, so strong that two villages were destroyed, and four others were severely damaged. There were many

ships that capsized or foundered on the rocks. Of a reported five or six hundred passengers and crew, only four souls survived.

Stranger still, these four passengers were related to each other and in the same line of work. They were in service to the law. They were lawyers. Snippy, Snide, Snaggy and Dreadful had embarked on a long-deserved vacation from their distant home when their ship foundered in a storm. (Since there were no planes at that time, boats and ships were the best way for long distance traveling.)

You might say, "oh my gosh!" What perfect names for lawyers! Well, that's what they thought. However, when they were all young lawyers, they seemed to be taken advantage of because they weren't cut-throat nor did they use tactics that so often give lawyers a bad reputation. They simply and truly wanted to do the best for their clients. Snippy, Snide, Snaggy and Dreadful were nicknames given to them as young

children for an odd physical or character trait.
Ironically, their nicknames made them appear
tougher than they actually were, so they decided to
use them professionally.

Snippy, Snide, Snaggy and Dreadful wound up on the
rocky shore near the capital city, Agar, of the Empire
of Agaragar. It was there when that terrible storm
was over, that they were discovered tied to the ship's
mast unconscious and close to death. A young
villager who had been collecting flotsam along the
shore saw them and got help to take them to the local
medicine woman who, after a time, was able to bring
them back to health with herbal soups and aromatic
essences. As Snippy, Snide, Snaggy and Dreadful
recovered they began to explore the city, and
encounter its citizens, many of whom had never met
anyone who spoke another language. The locals
believed them to be idiots speaking gibberish.

Snippy, Snide, Snaggy and Dreadful, highly
intelligent, well-read and well-traveled as they were,
began to learn the language of the realm and soon
word reached the Emperor Fergie about the strangers
in the city who were, to say the least. . . peculiar.
Some even spoke the word "inhuman." Fergie, always
the curious one, sent out word to bring the four to
him for questioning. This is where Fergie's quest for

justice took a giant leap. With the help of the knowledge and experience of the four legal beagles, who were now able to speak the local language, new ideas began to form in the Emperor's mind. Snippy, Snide, Snaggy and Dreadful were appointed as the Emperor's justice counsellors and eventually set up an office for their law practice. They even founded the first, sanctioned School of Law. There were only two members in the first class - both women.

It was at this time that Albert and Percival entered the capital city where Normals, in general, didn't pay much attention to them. Even better, they weren't immediately given the bum's rush. They checked in to a Dwarf-friendly inn, got a good night's sleep and began the search for the cousins from their mother's side of the family.

Noodle, Hinkelberry and Cupcake were the three cousins who resided in the city. They were the only members of the family who would still speak to them after the catastrophic family split twenty years before. Don't ask about why the family split; that is for another story. At any rate, Albert and Percival needed help to get around the city safely and, perhaps, find someone to introduce them to anyone who might be able to help with their predicament to rescue Snow.

Thus, began the search for their cousins' whereabouts. Of course, the best places to get information about Dwarves are the pubs that sell a certain type of mead made with honey from the far

northwestern part of the Empire. That did limit the
number to only about, er . . . two hundred pubs.
Now, Albert and Percival had no idea how very many
pubs there were, so they optimistically started
looking.

First stop, the Thistle and Dog, brought some
immediate success with a few general directions.
However, the capital
city was notably
large with
dizzyingly twisted
streets and
confusing alleys
where one might
become seriously
lost. They often had
to ask for further
help and sadly, more
often than not,
some Normals
would send them on
wild goose chases.
It took another day
and a half, with all
the bad directions
and back-tracking
though some dark

and often dangerous parts of the city, to find their relatives.

At a point when the brothers were at their wit's end, as they entered an intersection they were set upon by some ruffians. Albert applied reason but Percival just said, "Look, I am a really angry Little Person and work in a mine ten hours a day so, if you really want to mess with us, bring it on!" And the three men backed away. This unnerving incident left them hungry and thirsty, so on they went to find an appropriate pub where they satisfied both needs.

Serendipitously, upon exiting the pub, they spotted a large wooden sign on the building across the street imprinted in gold letters that read, NOODLE HINKELBERRY and CUPCAKE: Finders and Investigators.

 Apparently, in the past ten years since Albert and Percival had last seen them, Noodle, Hinkelberry and Cupcake had become private investigators of note, and were well-known in city circles, especially among the frequenters of those specialty pubs for the Dwarf community. So, instead of weeks, it only took a few days to find their cousins. At last they were standing in front of the building where they would get the best help possible. They were going to find Snow.

Let us look back a bit to the history of these found-
again cousins. Noodle, Hinkelberry and their sister
Cupcake were always a little different from the rest of
the family which began to show at early ages.
Cupcake was not fond of playing with dolls or doing
what was considered "woman's work." Although she
never shirked her duty to the family, there was a time
when it became almost more than she could bear.

She much preferred to wander in the woods
searching for stuff. She never knew what she might
find, but she usually found SOMETHING.

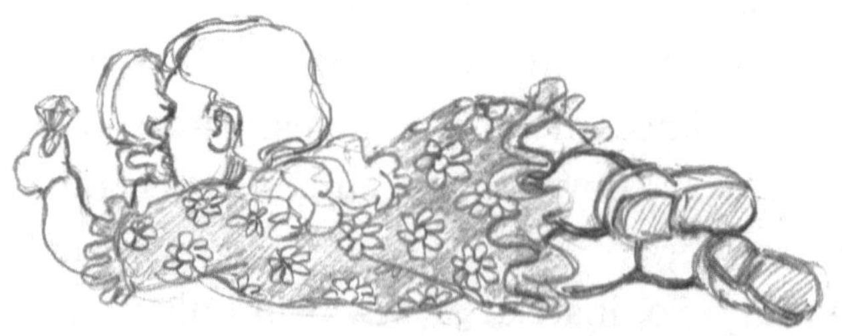

Her younger brothers seemed to follow suit when they got old enough to wander with her. Her talent for finding things was often a blessing as it came in handy when something or SOMEONE was lost. Ninety-nine times out of a hundred, Cupcake and her brothers would find whatever or whomever was missing. It just seemed to be a knack that they shared.

Eventually, their ability for finding things and people was not a blessing at all, particularly for Cupcake. When she came of age she was expected to marry, and the boys were expected to go into the family business – mining. This was not a direction with which Cupcake was comfortable, so when she turned sixteen, she slipped away from the family home in the dark of night. The brothers followed and, when they caught up with her, argued persuasively until they convinced their sister that they should stick together. After a time, they found their way to the capital city. Though it was tough for a while, in time they became well known for their talents. Realizing they could make "finding" into a good business, they began N. H. & C., Finders and Investigators and "found" it to be quite lucrative.

Meanwhile, back at the castle, it had become obvious to Snow that the Prince's family didn't think much of her. On top of that, they had no appreciation of her ability to think beyond what she might wear on any given day. Well, we all know that she could but, since she was confined to her room, with the door locked and guarded, except when she ate with the Prince and his family, it never occurred to any of them to converse with Snow at mealtimes or to visit her in her room, so they never suspected how very bright and capable she was. And certainly, not one of them thought about the large open window in the room, the balcony conveniently below it and the mere thirty-foot drop to the ground. But Snow DID think about it.

It had been over a month since she had recovered her wits completely, and Snow had had plenty of time to formulate her plan to escape. Her plan was simple and dangerous, it included making a rope from her sheets, climbing down to ground level, making her way through the city without notice and finding her way to safety and Percival. Since preparations for the wedding were speedily underway, time was of the essence.

As we know in most stories about Snow, she is made out to be a vapid, thoughtless, helpless thing. Well, NOT THIS SNOW WHITE. In our story Snow was in very good physical condition. After working with Percival and his brothers, one might even say she was buff. So, on one moonless night, she tied her rope to the balcony, hiked up her skirt and shinnied her way to the ground. As she made her way into the forest, Snow appropriated some boy's clothes from a clothesline. They looked to be a good fit and, as soon as she felt safe enough, she changed out of her dress and buried it. Wearing the purloined garments with her hair tucked into a cap, she was able to pass as a young boy.

Snow knew she was going to need things for her escape that she couldn't get hold of before she fled the castle. She would need things like clothes and maybe some tools. So, for this potential she took a small bag of gems she had been given to wear at meals and formal dinners. Snow felt a little better taking things from people who probably couldn't afford to lose them when she left a small gem at each of the places where she found items she needed.

This way the owners were compensated with something more valuable than what they had lost.

Off into the deep woods she went. You may ask, was she afraid to be all alone in the deepest of forests where few men would choose to go? I'd be lying if I said no. Of course, she was but, considering the alternatives, she knew she was much better off to chance the dangers she might face there.

Remember all the time she was with the Seven before her poisoning? She wasn't simply cleaning and cooking. Each one of the brothers took time to teach her woodcraft, so she wasn't without resources. She could live for years on her own if need be. She also knew how to cover her trail.

Let's return to Snow's family castle. You might think that all this time, Snow's stepmother was content thinking Snow was dead. Well, you would be wrong in your thinking. After having observed the delivery of the poison apple and watching Snow eat it. She went back to the castle and began planning her own Coronation.

During the time Snow was in the deep sleep, apparently she was not detectable by the mirror, so when her vain stepmother once again asked the mirror who was the most beautiful in the world, it would answer, "You are, oh great Queen." (Even though she wasn't Queen she demanded that the mirror referred to her as Queen.) And so, the coronation preparations were well underway when Snow was awakened and carried away by the Prince.

By way of reports from travelers, the Queen learned that a wedding of monumental proportions was being planned in the neighboring kingdom, and that the bride-to-be was astoundingly beautiful. Hearing that,

Snow's evil stepmother rushed to the mirror (talk about being insecure!). Addressing the mirror, she cried, "Mirror, Mirror, let me see, is this new girl lovelier than me?" And to her amazement and horror, the mirror replied,

"By far is she lovelier than thee,
 but not new to you is she.
She is known to you but
not the same!
 Snow White is her given name."

"NOOOOOOOOOOOOOOOO!!!!" shrieked the Queen and stomped her foot so hard she shrieked in pain, "OOOOOOOOOOOOOOOOOOOuch!!!!!" and hobbled to her bed to scream into her pillow. Little did she know that when the mirror responded to her question, Snow was deep in the woods, dressed as a boy and completely filthy, head to toe. Did the mirror know something?

We return now to Albert and Percival. They had explained the situation   and were in process with Noodle, Hinkelberry and Cupcake brain-storming about what to do next. Suddenly, Noodle slapped his head and shouted, "Snippy, Snide, Snaggy and Dreadful!"

 Albert and Percival thought he had lost his mind, but his siblings, at once, cheered, "Of course! Why didn't we think of them sooner?"

 As we know, but Albert and Percival did not, Snippy, Snide, Snaggy and Dreadful were lawyers and confidants of the Emperor and, also, friends of Hinkleberry, Noodle and Cupcake. Immediately, they sent a note by runner to Snippy, Snide, Snaggy and Dreadful (from now on, to be referred to as S. S. S. & D., Ltd.) for a meeting the very next day. After all that brainwork, a serious meal and "more mead" was called for. To the pub they went!

At the appointed time, the meeting with the learned lawyers took place, introductions were made, pleasantries exchanged and the story told. S. S. S. & D. could easily see the injustice and, of course, the crime of attempted murder. They proceeded to set up an audience with Emperor Fergie.

The plot thickens.

Elsewhere, late on a beautiful morning the self-centered Prince went to check in on Snow and he noticed that her uneaten breakfast was still on the tray outside her door. After knocking, and a few "Good mornings" and "Dearests," he finally unlocked the door, only to find the room empty with the makeshift rope still hanging loosely from the window! "NOOOOOOOOOOOOOOOOOOO!!!!!" he screamed. Apparently, this is what evil people do when their plans are foiled.

Thinking the worst, at least, the worst for him (who in her right mind wouldn't want to be married to him or would run away from a life of great luxury?) he raised the alarm, "Snow has been abducted! Guards, Guards! Search the grounds and if that fails, go house to house throughout the Kingdom to find her. She must be found, and her kidnappers executed . . . And look for those damned Dwarves!"

It took almost a week for a search of the grounds and the city. Only then did they think to search the outskirts. No one imagined that she had escaped on her own. No woman could do what a man could, much less a refined princess like Snow White. How deeply they underestimated her and, by the way, all women! But that's a subject for a very different narrative.

Marcus, James, Bertram, Emilio and Zachary, the five
brothers who stayed behind to work the mine while
Albert and Percival went off in search of Snow,
learned through the Dwarf grapevine that Snow had
gone missing and that the Prince's soldiers were
coming after them. They made haste to hide
themselves at the mine making sure they cleared out
all of their valuables. They did, however, leave some
old furniture behind for the soldiers to smash,
because that's what soldiers do when their task is
frustrated, and they have an angry and murderous
Prince to answer to.

The soldiers did as was expected. In addition to
breaking the law by crossing into a neighboring
kingdom without permission and by destroying
property of subjects who were residents of that
neighboring kingdom! Ooh, golly, the violations
were mounting up fast.

You might wonder what's been happening to Snow
while all of this was transpiring. Well, she was living

quite well deep in the forest. Of course, she made sure to go in the opposite direction from what, she knew, would be the direction the Prince would take. She went boldly, straight into the Forbidden Forest. While no one was actually forbidden to go there, it was.... well ... so scary... so deep.... and dark ... it was ... just FORBIDDING. Goosebumps, ya know?

As she slept one morning, the birds were sweetly singing their dawn beginning-of-day songs and the sun was filtering through the trees. She stretched and sighed a contented wakening sigh, thoroughly enjoying the birds' twitterings. When she opened her eyes to meet the dawn, she met the face of a man instead, a man with a scraggly beard and long snarled hair. He was leaning over her observing her carefully. Quickly, she rolled over, grabbed her knife, and jumped into a threatening and defensive position.

"Who are you? What do you want?" she shouted. "See," he said, a bit shaken, "I'm way ahead of you. I know who you are and what you want. Also, if I had wanted to harm you, I could have done it while you were sleeping AND taken your knife, as well. So, you can relax, and maybe we can talk? Yes?   My name is ..."

Well, we'll get to that later. It's enough to know that he took Snow in and took care of her and taught her more about woodcraft, and a little more about human nature.

At the same time Percival and Albert regaled their tale in a private meeting with the Emperor Fergie the Just. True to his name, Fergie sent some of his guards to the Prince's castle with Albert and Percival, along with Noodle, Hinkelberry and Cupcake, to get Snow released. And while there, he commanded the guards to arrest the Prince for kidnapping. He further directed them to warn the King and Queen to behave more like true rulers and let them know, in no uncertain terms, that they would likely lose their kingdom if they behaved otherwise. So there! However, when they arrived, guess what? Ah, but you already know. No Snow White!

Predictably, not wanting to raise the ire of the Emperor, the King tried to explain the situation. The Prince added, with sly winks that made it look like he had a really bad facial tic, that Snow had wanted to be there with him, and her disappearance was all the fault of "those dirty midgets."

Contriving a sorrowful look and begging for sympathy for the missing love of his life, the Prince explained how after several weeks of searching, and even tearing apart the "dirty midgets'" house, they had not found even a bit of hair from Snow's head. "I have been so distraught since she disappeared," he sobbed.

 "Excuse me," spoke up Albert. "Did you get permission to enter the domain of another kingdom or break into our house and tear it apart?"

"Oh, no, we didn't need to. Royal business," retorted the Prince. The King thumped the back of the Prince's head and hissed, "Shut up!"

At this point, Percival strode over to the Prince saying, "This is for calling us midgets!" and kicked the Prince in the shin – HARD! And as the Prince bent over to grab his leg, Percival growled, "And this is for kidnapping Snow!" With that, Percival landed a perfect uppercut to the Prince's chiseled chin that set him on his backside knocking him out cold. Hah!

"It's a good thing we're finders." said Cupcake. "We're on the case." Noodle, Hinkelberry and Cupcake then proceeded, each with one of the

Emperor's soldiers, to search for clues, returning at the end of the day to piece them together.

The next morning, (the Dwarves were all, grudgingly, given beds for the night) all the cousins, with ten of the soldiers, went into the Forbidden Forest, hoping Snow would be found and praying that she would be alive.

Two days had passed when they stepped cautiously onto the grounds of the old woodsman's home where he and Snow were calmly talking. Upon hearing steps, Snow looked up to see Percival beaming with the most glorious smile she had ever seen on his face. They ran to each other, Snow sliding down to her knees to be at Percival's face level. Such a hug the world has never seen!

And, for the first time, Snow and Percival kissed. We can tell you that it was well worth the wait.

Everyone else sort of shuffled their feet and looked everywhere but at the two in their joyful embrace. Snow and Percival whispered sweet words to each other, kissed some more then turned and smiled to the group around them. The only one not smiling ear to ear was the hermit woodsman. But, after observing Snow and Percival, so obviously in love, he too began to smile as broadly as the others. There followed introductions all around, including the soldiers.

It was then with downcast eyes that Percival said, "Snow, as much as I love you, I must ask, are you sure you're willing to give up the rich, pampered and cultured life of a princess to be with a lowly, hardworking miner in the woods?"

Snow softly smiled at him and said, "I've been keeping something from you my love. I already am a princess. My father was King, and my stepmother is setting herself up as queen in my stead. And yes, I would rather spend my life with you in a simple hut than with that oaf, Charming."

This set Percival back on his heels and, then in a kind of daze said, "Well, in that case, I guess it's time we got you home. All the others just stood back with startled looks on their faces. Curiously, the hermit just continued to smile.

After a good meal, great comradery and a good night's sleep, they arose the next morning to make their way back to Snow's kingdom.

Before departing, Snow gave the woodsman an affectionate hug, thanked him for his kindness and said, "Goodbye." Meanwhile, though Snow was looking forward to going home, it was with some trepidation because of the upcoming confrontation with her stepmother. The hermit interrupted her thoughts and said, "I'd like to come along, if that's alright with you."

Snow replied, "Of course you may, but I don't know why you would want to." Why would he, indeed?

So, off they all went to take care of Snow's stepmother who had already held her coronation and was reportedly even more vile to her subjects than ever before, if that can be believed.

It caused quite a stir in the kingdom when Snow, five dwarves and, now, one hundred of the Emperor's guards rode into the city on their way to the castle. Word spread quickly ahead to the castle. However, the "Queen" had left word that "under NO circumstances, am I to be disturbed." By the time someone among the servants got brave enough to disturb her, she had just enough time to ready herself to be standing in front of the mirror when Snow burst in to confront her.

"What's the meaning of this?" shouted the "Queen."

Without hesitation, Snow grabbed a stool and threw it against the mirror which smashed into a million pieces. Well, no one actually counted the pieces, but it was a sure thing the mirror would never be the same. Snow then strode over to her stepmother and punched her, very hard, in the nose. (And now you know why her nose looked the way it did when she got older. You know, kind of like a fairy tale witch?) "How dare you strike the Queen!"

"You're not the Queen. I am," said Snow with a calm and steady look into her stepmother's eyes that were now beginning to tear up and swell. "I became Queen during my long sleep."

"But you were dead!" sputtered the "Queen."

"And so, it seemed," replied Snow, "but not quite, and that fact proves three things. One, I was not dead. I became Queen upon my coming of age. Two, because of that, you could never be Queen. And, three, because it was you who gave me the poison apple, you are under arrest for attempted murder."

It was, at this moment, that the hermit stepped forward causing Snow's stepmother to have the most horrified look of recognition on her face. When the hermit woodsman spoke, all were silent. His words were like a lightning flash.

 "All that is true to a point Snow, all except for you becoming Queen on your birthday."

 Snow looked at him with a deep frown, "Why?"

"Well, I would have to be dead for either of you to become Queen, because I am your father. I am the King!" With that announcement, the "Queen" dropped to the floor in a dead faint. All Snow could do was stand in shock, eyes and mouth wide open. "You see Snow," he said, "when I went hunting, so long ago, at the urging of your stepmother, the same man who was sent to kill you with the poison apple, had been sent to kill me. He didn't have the heart to do it and I felt it wise to live as a hermit while keeping track of the goings on in the kingdom. I knew nothing of the mirror and the power it gave to her, but I was also under its spell until you awoke, and I was able to see the whole picture. For some reason, you were immune to the power she had and were protected from the deadly effects of the poison in the apple."

Everyone present at that moment, bowed to the King and to the Princess Snow White. The stepmother was hustled out of the room and taken straight to the prison tower to await her trial.

It was then that the King reclaimed his throne and proceeded to undo all the mischief that had been done by his now ex-wife. At this time, we must also report that the wicked stepmother (as she was known from then on) managed to escape the tower and travel to Bavaria where, it is rumored, that she built a house made of gingerbread. Could it be?

Snow and Percival were married in the most beautiful and unusual ceremony, attended by Percival's brothers and hundreds of Little People and Normals. Emperor Fergie gladly presided over the festivities and, of course, also in attendance, were Noodle, Hinkelberry and Cupcake and the lawyers, Snippy, Snide, Snaggy and Dreadful.

Albert and the rest of the brothers went back to the cottage in the woods to continue life as before this adventure began, making frequent visits to the castle. The surrounding area became a Mecca for Little People and others who often are considered, in the world, as outcasts.

As time wore on, Snow and Percival brought into the world children of beautiful sizes and shapes and, eventually, became the most amazing Queen and King.

Of course, they lived happily ever after … Well, mostly.

And, really, is it ever

THE END?

Fred Zimmerman was born and raised in Southwest Florida. He has lived for varying lengths of time in California, Maine, Connecticut and is now living in Western North Carolina with his wife Laurie. He is self-employed as a carpenter/handyman and has been an electrician, plumber, merchandiser at a big box store and floor sales at another. He also was a mime, dancer and actor all of which he would have preferred spending much more time doing. This is not his first foray into writing, just his first completion.